Mini BUS

My Little Book of Opposites

Reprinted in 2016

An imprint of Om Books International

Corporate & Editorial Office
A 12, Sector 64, Noida 201 301
Uttar Pradesh, India
Phone: +91 120 477 4100
Email: editorial@ombooks.com
Website: www.ombooksinternational.com

Sales Office
107, Ansari Road, Darya Ganj
New Delhi 110 002, India
Phone: +91 11 4000 9000
Fax: +91 11 2327 8091
Email: sales@ombooks.com
Website: www.ombooks.com

ISBN : 978-93-84119-87-4

Printed in India

10 9 8 7 6 5 4 3 2

My Little Book of

Opposites

Om KIDZ

An imprint of Om Books International

Big

Basketball

Small

Cricket Ball

Old

Old Shoe

New Shoe

Full

Full Glass

Empty

Empty Glass

Fast

Rabbit

Slow

Snail

Many

Many Puppies

Few Puppies

Heavy

Bus

Light

Cycle

Open

Open Box

Close

Closed Box

Wide

Wide Door

Narrow

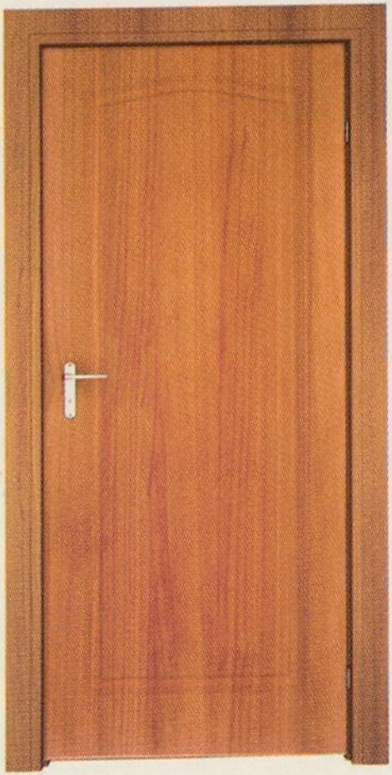

Narrow Door

Long

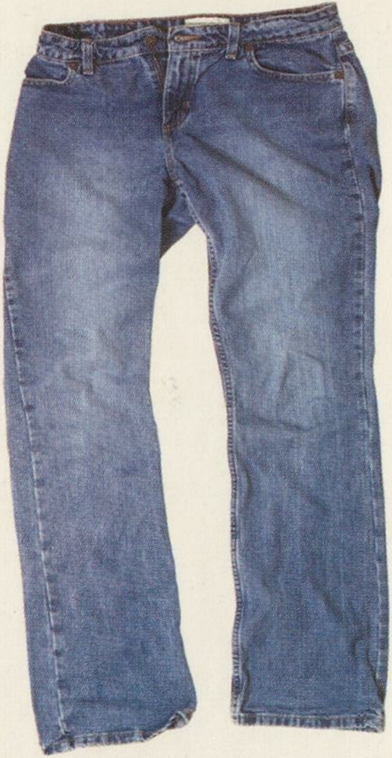

Trousers

Short

Shorts

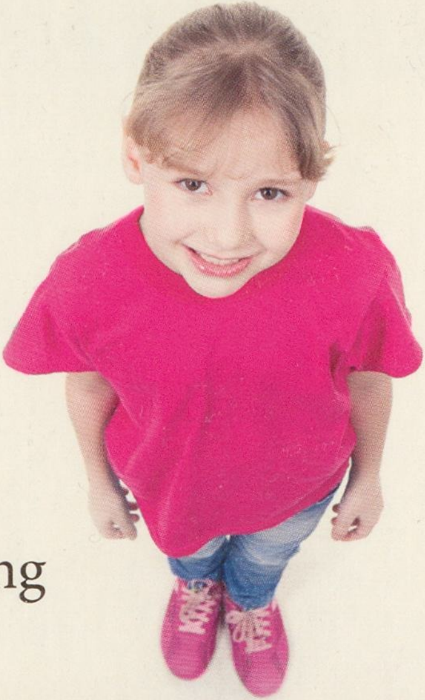

Looking
Up

Looking
Down

Hot

Hot Coffee

Cold Coffee

Fat

Fat Dog

Thin

Thin Dog

Candies

Sour

Lemons

My Little Book of Opposites

Om KIDZ

An imprint of Om Books International

ISBN 978-93-84119-87-4

9 789384 119874

www.ombooksinternational.com

Om KIDZ